❧ STORYTIME CLASSICS ❧

LITTLE WOMEN

by Louisa May Alcott
retold by Janet Allison Brown • illustrated by Dinah Dryhurst

Puffin Books

PUFFIN BOOKS
Published by the Penguin Group
Penguin Putnam Books for Young Readers, 345 Hudson Street, New York, New York 10014, U.S.A.
Penguin Books Ltd, 27 Wrights Lane, London W8 5TZ, England
Penguin Books Australia Ltd, Ringwood, Victoria, Australia
Penguin Books Canada Ltd, 10 Alcorn Avenue, Toronto, Ontario, Canada M4V 3B2
Penguin Books (N.Z.) Ltd, 182-190 Wairau Road, Auckland 10, New Zealand

Penguin Books Ltd, Registered Offices: Harmondsworth, Middlesex, England

First published in Great Britain by Breslich & Foss, 2001
Published simultaneously by Viking and Puffin Books,
divisions of Penguin Putnam Books for Young Readers, 2001

10 9 8 7 6 5 4 3 2 1

LIBRARY OF CONGRESS CATALOGING-IN-PUBLICATION DATA
Brown, Janet Allison.
Little women / by Louisa May Alcott ; illustrated by Dinah Dryhurst ;
re-told by Janet Allison Brown.
p.   cm.
Summary: A simple retelling of the adventures of the four March sisters
living in New England during the time of the Civil War.
ISBN 0-670-89912-7 (hardcover) — ISBN 0-14-131202-5 (pbk.)
[1. Sisters—Fiction. 2. Family life—New England—Fiction. 3. New
England—Fiction.] I. Alcott, Louisa May, 1832–1888. Little women. II.
Dryhurst, Dinah, ill. III. Title.
PZ7.B814185 Li 2001 [Fic]—dc21 00-011883

Printed in Belgium

Louisa May Alcott
1832–1888

Louisa May Alcott, who wrote this story, was the second of four sisters—just like Jo in *Little Women*. Many of the adventures in *Little Women* took place in her own life, and she based the four March girls on herself and her three sisters. Louisa wrote stories all her life, including three more books about Meg, Jo, Beth, and Amy (*Good Wives, Little Men,* and *Jo's Boys*).

One cold evening just before Christmas, the four March sisters gathered round the fire to hear Mrs. March read a letter from Father, who was away in the army. Their mother—the girls called her *Marmee*—sat in the big chair, with Beth at her feet, Meg and Amy on either arm, and Jo leaning on the back.

"Will he be home soon?" asked Beth, with a quiver in her voice.

"Not for many months, dear," sighed Marmee.

Gentle Beth was everyone's favorite. She was shy, and liked staying at home with her family. Meg, the oldest sister, was fair and pretty and ladylike. Brown-haired Jo was a tomboy who loved to read and planned to be a great writer someday. And Amy, the baby of the family, was a most important person—in her own opinion, at least!

On Christmas morning, Marmee said, "Girls, not far from here is a poor family. They have no food or fire, and are freezing. Will you take them your breakfast as a Christmas present?"

Their own family was quite poor, and the girls thought longingly of their delicious breakfast. But they were all good hearted, so each of them cheerfully took up a dish and set off.

"I shall take the cream and muffins," said Amy, trying hard to be generous.

Later on Christmas Day, they dressed up in fancy costumes and put on a play for their friends. Afterward there was a big surprise—a Christmas supper, with ice cream and cake!

"Mr. Laurence sent it when he heard that you gave away your breakfast," explained Marmee.

Rich old Mr. Laurence lived next door. The girls hardly knew him, but they *did* know that he had a grandson they had never met.

One evening, Mr. Laurence invited Meg and Jo to a party. Meg was very excited, but Jo would rather have stayed home to finish her story. She agreed to go, but instead of joining in, she hid behind a curtain to peep out at everyone.

Unfortunately, someone else had the same idea, and Jo found herself face to face with Mr. Laurence's grandson! "Call me Laurie," he said, smiling at her. He was so friendly that Jo couldn't help liking him. They had great fun together, spying on the other guests and dancing up and down the hallway.

After that, the girls often waved to Laurie across the hedge between their houses. One snowy afternoon, Jo spotted him at his upstairs window. He looked pale and ill.

"Shall I come and read to you?" she called up. Laurie nodded, and within minutes Jo stood in the Laurence's hall with a dish of pudding and Beth's three kittens to cheer him up.

"I was feeling lonely until you came!" said Laurie gratefully.

While Jo and Laurie were getting to know each other, another more unusual friendship was developing. At first Beth was afraid of old Mr. Laurence, but when he invited her over to play his lovely piano, she could not resist.

Soon Beth was tiptoeing over to the big house every day, and Mr. Laurence always stopped what he was doing to listen to her playing.

One day when Beth came back from a walk, she spied her sisters waving and calling out of the window.

"Come quick," they called. "The old gentleman has given you a piano!"

Beth could hardly believe her ears.

Amy was feeling left out—everyone seemed to have new friends and fun except her. So the next time Jo and Laurie went skating on the river, she followed them.

At first Jo ignored her, but suddenly she heard a scream and turned to see Amy fall through the ice. Jo's heart stood still with fear. "Quick!" cried Laurie, rushing past her. "Bring a rail from the fence!" Together, they rescued Amy from the freezing water, and the two girls clung to one another. "I nearly lost you!" sobbed Jo.

At last the summer arrived. The girls invited
Laurie to join their private club—the Pickwick
Club—in which they all had secret names and
wrote a newspaper.

Laurie set up a "pretend" mailbox in the hedge between the houses, which they used to send things back and forth. They had picnics, went rowing, played croquet, and told stories.

In between, Jo spent a lot of time reading in the apple tree and writing stories up in the attic. By the end of the summer she had produced a fine collection, full of beautiful heroines, wonderful heroes, and wicked villains.

One day, she climbed out of her window clutching a bundle, and ran off into town on a secret errand.

On the way home, she met Laurie. "I've left two stories with a newspaper man," she told him. "It's a secret—but he might print them!"

Laurie and Jo raced home through the falling leaves—and a few days later, to everyone's surprise, two stories appeared in the newspaper, written by "Miss Josephine March"!

Everyone was celebrating Jo's success when a telegram arrived for Marmee.

It was bad news. "Your husband is very ill. Come at once." Suddenly the day seemed to darken. Marmee held out her arms and cried, "I shall go immediately, but it may be too late!" There was no time for tears—everyone was too busy helping Marmee get ready for the journey.

"How can I help?" thought Jo. She slipped out to the hairdresser, and let him cut off her beautiful brown hair to make a wig. He gave her $25, and she took it home to help pay for Marmee's train ticket. Then they all went out to wave Marmee off.

While Marmee was gone, the girls worked hard and waited for news. They missed her and worried about Father, but everyone did their best. Beth looked after some children with scarlet fever, but she was not strong and soon became sick herself.

As the weather grew colder, Meg and Jo tried to nurse Beth, but she got sicker and sicker. At last the doctor said, "You must send for your mother." Jo ran through the snow with a telegram to call Marmee home. Then she sat down and cried.

A few days later, there was a sound of bells at the door, and Laurie's voice cried, "Girls, she's come! She's come!" Marmee was home and in no time Beth began to improve.

Now, as another Christmas grew near, they worried only about their father.

Then something wonderful happened. After their presents were opened on Christmas Day, Laurie said, "Here's another Christmas present for the March family!"—and in walked Father!

There never was such a Christmas dinner as they had that day, with a fat turkey and everyone gathered around the table: Marmee and Father, Meg, Jo, Beth, and Amy, with Mr. Laurence and Laurie.

"Everyone looks so happy, I don't believe things could get any better!" said Jo. And they all agreed it was their best Christmas ever.